39331

DEMCO

This book was a
gift to Butterfield
School Library to
honor the birthday of

Scott Ruffell

June 16, 1990

Skeleton Crew

ALLAN AHLBERG · ANDRÉ AMSTUTZ

Mulberry Books · New York

Text copyright © 1992 by Allan Ahlberg. Illustrations copyright © 1992 by André Amstutz. The right of Allan Ahlberg and André Amstutz to be identified as author and illustrator of this work has been asserted. First published in Great Britain in 1992 by William Heinemann Ltd, a division of Reed International Books. First published in the United States in 1992 in hardcover by Greenwillow Books and in paperback by Mulberry Books. All rights reserved. No part of this book may be reproduced or utilized in any form or by any means, electronic or mechanical, including photocopying, recording, or by any information storage and retrieval system, without permission in writing from the Publisher, Greenwillow Books, a division of William Morrow & Company, Inc., 1350 Avenue of the Americas, New York, NY 10019.
Produced by Mandarin; printed and bound in Hong Kong   First American Edition   10 9 8 7 6 5 4 3 2 1

Library of Congress Cataloging-in-Publication Data
Ahlberg, Allan.
    Skeleton crew / by Allan Ahlberg ;
pictures by André Amstutz.
        p.   cm.
    Summary: Three skeletons have a good time
on their sailing vacation, until their
boat is boarded by pirates.
    ISBN 0-688-11660-4
    [1. Skeleton—Fiction.   2. Sea stories.
3. Vacations—Fiction.   4. Humorous stories.]
I. Amstutz, André, ill.   II. Title.
PZ7.A2688Sk   1992   [E]—dc20
91-39161   CIP   AC

On a dark dark night,
on a dark dark sea,
in a dark dark boat
three skeletons float . . .

on a vacation.

The big one is dozing
in his deck chair.
"Zzz!"

Zzz!

The dog one is dozing
in his hammock.
"Zzz!"
The little one is fishing.

Zzz!

I've got a bite!

The little skeleton
catches a fish
and throws it back.

He catches a boot
and throws it back.

He catches an octopus . . .

and it throws <u>him</u> back.

Splash!

The next night
in the dark dark boat,
under the starry sky,
the big one has a try.

The big skeleton catches a little fish
and throws it back.
He catches a big fish and keeps it.
He catches a bigger fish . . .

And – "Yo – ho – ho!" –
he pirates come.

The pirates climb aboard
looking for treasure.
They steal the deck chair
and the hammock.

Bye-bye!

They steal the fishing rod
and the cat fish.
"Miaow!"
They steal . . . the boat!

That's a nice rod — I'll have that!

The next night . . .
nothing happens.

But the <u>next</u> night,
under a starry sky
and over the deep blue sea,
the skeletons spy . . . a tree.
"Yippee!"

Land ahoy!

On the island
the big skeleton
finds a parrot.
"Pretty Polly!"

The next night a lot happens.
A storm blows up.
The thunder crashes,
the lightning flashes,
the wind howls
and the dog howls, too.
"Howl!"

As quick as a blink
the raft is blown
across the foam . . .

The End (or is it?)

The End